A Perfect Gentooman

Sylvia Morrow

Content Notes

Surprise pregnancy, babies, alcohol, being uncomfortable with one's appearance, internalized ageism, arguing with a voice in your head, longing to have a child, head injury.

Cover by Unfortunate Reads

This story previously appeared in a slightly shorter form in the Matched By the Unicorn anthology.

The author does not support the use of generative AI in its current unethical form.

Chapter One
David

It happened again today.

Was a basketball this time. Couldn't help myself. Sat on top of it for two hours straight, thinking about what it would be like to have an egg of my own. An egg to keep warm. Swap duties with a mate. Just sitting on that ball daydreaming about such a life.

Never thought I'd be a broody man. The other gentoo penguin men warned me this day would come if I put off trying to find a mate for too long, but I was stubborn. Wanted to focus on work, on top of never really having much desire for a wife.

Now here I am, gazing longingly at volleyballs.

"David, my boy, where's your head at?" My best friend George interrupts my thoughts.

"Ah, sorry. Think I have to admit I've got the old egg fever. Can't believe it's finally happened." I pinch the bridge of my nose to calm the impending stress headache.

If my kind get stressed, things can go south quickly. Especially in public. *Calm your nerves, David.*

"Well, what did you expect? You're pushing forty. The rest of us have been mated since our twenties. Didn't think you'd make it this long, to be fair."

"What am I gonna do, George? How do I even find a gentoo woman my age who'd want to mate? I'm happy alone, damn it."

I lay back in the sand on the beach and look at the clouds. The weather here in Southern California is much different than back on the Falklands where I was born. Even after all these years, I'm not quite used to it. Still don't truly feel settled in. Maybe it's because I never really settled down.

The first wave of us penguin folk came here after a group of human tourists all instantly mate bonded with a group of gentoo at the same time. It was a strange event we just refer to as The Bonding. My father was a widower, taking care of me by himself. He instantly bonded with one of the women, Tina, and left the Falklands to join her in California. It was quite a shock, to say the least, to go from being in a small, isolated community of non-humans in the southern half of the world to a highly populated, warm, and sunny part of the north.

A bit of that northern sun shines in my eyes just now, causing me to squint against the brightness. I turn my head and see a set of sparkly purple toenails where there weren't any a moment before. I follow the legs attached upward to find a lovely lady with warm brown skin, curly hair, and a flashing grin.

"I heard you're looking for a mate," she says.

"That's true. Are you looking to fill the position?" I raise a brow. "Don't suppose I'm that lucky to have a prospect in the first thirty seconds of the search."

"Not me, no. Sorry," she laughs. "I'm Miriam, the matchmaker."

She sits next to me in the sand, and I sit up, shaking her hand as I go. There's a pleasant and powerful feeling about her that makes me want to lean in and listen to what she says. So, I do.

"Your friend George probably remembers me from when I ran a matchmaking website for non-humans. Now, I do everything through an app."

"Yeah, of course I remember," George says, eyes lighting up at the memory. "That's how I met Sally."

"This is the unicorn?" My eyebrows lift in surprise. I've heard about the unicorn matchmaker that can allegedly find anyone their perfect mate. Never expected that she'd help me, though.

"That's me. Would you like some help? All you need to do is download the app and wait for me to find your match. Easy as pie."

A volleyball soars past again, making my heart twinge with longing. But I'm old fashioned. If I'm going to mate, I want to meet a woman the proper way. Fall in love at first sight, just like my Mom and dad, then my stepmom and dad after that.

"I'm sorry. I don't think it's for me."

Miriam catches the next volleyball that soars past, gives it a few tosses, and shrugs her shoulders.

"Suit yourself."

Chapter Two

Sarah

"I'm not downloading a dating app. I'm too old for that stuff. Can't I just meet a guy the old-fashioned way?" I take a frustrated bite of string cheese. Yeah, I don't peel it into little strings. Just big chomps. I'm a monster like that.

"How will you meet someone when you spend all your time alone, at home?" my best friend, Mira, asks over video chat. We still talk a few times a week. Even after knowing each other for almost thirty years. "And you're not old, dumbass. Quit saying that. Thirty-seven is a perfectly fine age to get back into dating. Your ageism is showing."

"Okay, fine, I'm not old. I know that. I just don't want to be compared to little twenty-year-olds with perky boobs who've never birthed a child."

I, on the other hand, had a baby at seventeen. Recently, my son, Teddy, moved out of the house. I thought I might feel a sense of freedom, but all I feel is an empty nest.

"Then find someone who likes motherly types with squishy tits," Mira laughs. "I'm telling you, there's someone for everyone. Just go find a dating app that looks good and try it out. Use your internet safety skills, obviously."

I roll my eyes at her. "Obviously."

"Come on. You'll feel so much better when you get some good dick."

"Oh my God shut up," I snap.

"Make sure it's good dick, too. Like really assess the guy before you sleep with him to make sure he seems like he's not going to be a dud. I don't want your first time in years to be lame."

"Mira, I barely even remember what a dick looks like at this point. I'm not going to be able to tell whether or not someone is good at it before we're in bed!"

"Well, what's the point otherwise? Hey, okay, make sure he licks the kitty. That way you know he–"

"I don't wanna talk anymore," I whine.

"Why so shy all of a sudden? You talk about sex to me all the time!"

"About *your* sex life. Not *mine.* I don't want to talk about kitty licking when I haven't even made a date. I mean first things first; I'll think about maybe buying underwear that aren't five years old if I get a second date." I wink at the camera.

Finally, I get her to change the subject. Our conversation goes for almost another hour before we run out of steam. But before we end it, she tries again to convince me to download a dating app.

I think about it again, but it's just not for me.

"Sorry. Can't do it. Not yet. Just give me a few days to think it over. Right now, I'm going to go meet Teddy at the beach."

Chapter Three
David

S and starts to work its way into the back of my swim shorts somehow. Don't know how I'm going to get the sand out of my crack without anyone noticing. Beach is too crowded. But goddamn, does it itch.

I take a long swig of my beer and look at George, who seems to be engrossed in a conversation with his Sally as they walk away to grab some snacks at a kiosk. On the other side of me is a young man setting up an umbrella, paying no attention to what I'm doing. The volleyball court is in front of me, and thankfully they seem to be occupied with their game. The open ocean's behind me. Now's my chance to get the sand out of my arse before anyone notices.

I do a casual single leg shimmy first, but it doesn't help. A little shake of the hips does better, but still no luck. The damn sweat from this California heat has trapped the sand to my crack. I look around one more time to make sure no one is paying attention, and then scratch away. On the outside of the fabric, of course. I'm not an animal. Usually.

The feeling of the sand falling away is bliss. Goodbye itchiness. I close my eyes and sigh.

WHAM!

Straight in the face, I get slammed hard enough to knock me backward. Thank the lord I'm in the sand so my fall is soft, but my head is ringing when I open my eyes.

I hear the bells of angels get louder. Feel the strokes of their feathers against my skin. Have I gone to Heaven?

No. But there's certainly a goddess here in front of me.

The bells transform into a voice asking me if I'm alright. The feathers are a soft hand stroking my forehead and hair, checking for injury. The goddess is the most beautiful woman I've ever seen. In the crook of her arm, she holds an egg. *Is it my egg?*

I blink hard against the sun. *What the hell is wrong with me? That's not an egg, it's a volleyball.*

"Sir? Are you alright?" she asks again, worry etched on her freckled features.

"Yeah, sorry. Got a good smack there. I'm fine now. Thanks. Don't worry about it." I hold a hand up as I sit and wave off the issue before she thinks about apologizing. She doesn't have anything to be sorry about. Accidents happen, after all.

She looks at the ball, looks at me. Her green eyes open wide as she shakes her head from side to side.

"Oh! It wasn't me that did it. It was that lady. I'm pretty sure she was aiming for you if I'm being honest. Do you know her?" The woman looks worried as she points in the direction of the parking lot where another woman is walking away, too far away to chase after now.

A woman with curly hair and purple, sparkly toenails. *Damn unicorn.*

"Barely. She made me an offer I turned down," I grumble, as I rub a sore spot on the bridge of my nose. "Apparently, she doesn't take well to rejection."

"Mom! Who's your friend?" The young man setting up the umbrella shouts over to us. He has to be at least in his late teens, maybe even older. This is his mother?

"Oh, we just met!" She turns to me with a bright smile, showcasing slightly crooked teeth and adorable dimples. "What's your name?"

"Name's David. And yours?" I hold out my hand, which feels like an incredibly old-fashioned gesture, but also appropriate at the same time.

"Sarah." She waves over in the direction of the young man. "And that's my son, Teddy. Teddy, this is David. Pleased to meet you."

Sarah and I exchange handshakes before Teddy and I exchange waves. The son is keeping a watchful eye on the two of us, but not interrupting. Already I can tell he's a good lad.

The sun shines down on Sarah's ginger hair, making it glow almost gold. She's on her knees in a white swimsuit with a matching white wrap-around skirt thingy that I can already find myself wanting to tear off her wide hips. Lord, she's a looker.

"Do you spend a lot of time at the beach getting beat up by women?"

My face heats in embarrassment as I run my hand through my hair nervously. Of course, I meet the first woman who's tickled my fancy in ages after I've been knocked to the ground. Also, while scratching my arse.

"Not something I make a habit of. Trying something new today but I don't think it's for me. Live, you learn." I laugh nervously.

Sarah breaks into a fit of giggles, covering her crooked smile as she laughs. Her cleavage jiggles inside her swimsuit as she does, and I have to force myself to look away, so I don't stare. Even looking away, I have to fight off rogue thoughts of laying atop those soft pillows. I clear my throat and take a swig of my, unfortunately, warm beer.

"What brings you to the beach today? Family time?" I nod to Teddy, who's still got his eyes locked on us.

"Oh, yeah. We just sit on the beach a few times a week and chat about life. Been doing it since he was little. Helps him healthily express his feelings, if he wants to. If he doesn't feel up to chatting, we can just meditate and watch the water and enjoy the beautiful southern California weather."

She smiles with eyes that aren't really focused on me. It's the type of smile people get when they talk about something attached to years of important memories, love, and history. This is something that tells me key bits of who she is. She cares about family. Cares for children. Resolving feelings. Communication. The beauty of nature.

I think I really like this woman.

My stomach feels like it's dropping out of my feet, and I'm suddenly so dizzy the world is spinning around me. Lights flash like crazy before my eyes, my heart races, and all I can think is *Sarah, Sarah, Sarah.*

Oh God.

It's the mate bond. I've found my mate.

Chapter Four
Sarah

Wow, I didn't know a volleyball could hurt someone this badly. This man must be seriously injured. I have to get him some help. Cradling David's head in my arms, I wave Teddy over in a near panic.

"David, hold on, okay? I'll get you some help. We'll get you an ambulance. You must have a concussion or something, gosh."

"What the hell's going on, Mom? Get away from that strange guy." He tugs my arm, but I yank it away with a frown.

"Ted, you know better than that. This man needs help. Now, get your phone and call for help!"

"Wait, no," David croaks out. "I'm fine. Please don't call an ambulance. My friend is here somewhere close by, George. He's a doctor. He'll be back."

I look around and don't see another man nearby. But I see a second cooler and a beach blanket. Someone who was here recently, and likely will be back shortly. He's telling the truth. Still, I don't like leaving him in this condition. He looks dazed and confused. I'm staying right here until I know he's okay.

"Are you sure you're alright? I'm going to just wait here, okay?" I nervously chew on my lip and look around again for his friend. There's a couple in the distance coming this way. Maybe that's them.

"That's fine. Very fine," mumbles David as he snuggles closer against me, eyes closed.

"No, no, don't go to sleep! You're not supposed to sleep if you have a concussion!" I yelp.

"Want me to smack him, Mom? That'll wake him up," Teddy grumbles.

I give Teddy a sharp look at the same time David opens his eyes with a smile.

"I'm not sleeping. Only relaxed. What a day," he laughs softly to himself before closing his eyes again.

"Mom, I think he's crazy," Teddy whispers.

"Teddy–"

"David?" One of the people in the couple shouts as he runs down the beach toward us. "David, are you alright?"

In a moment, a clean-cut, blonde man kneels before the slightly more frazzled, black-haired David. The man is looking into David's pupils, asking him questions about how he feels. This must be George, the doctor friend.

When David doesn't reply much, I explain to George about the volleyball and the strange, delayed reaction.

"David, what's going on now?" George asks, more softly than before. "It's not the volleyball, is it?

When David huffs out a soft laugh, Teddy and I look at one another with wrinkled brows of confusion.

"No," David says, "it's not. It's the whole mate thing. Can you believe it, George?"

David looks down at the sand, and his glazed eyes focus for a moment on something. He reaches down with a shaky hand and picks up a smooth, blue piece of sea glass. It looks like a wonderfully beautiful precious stone, a lovely find in a strange situation.

"Good timing then," David laughs. "For you."

He sets the sea glass in my open palm, closes his eyes, and promptly falls asleep.

Chapter Five
David

Oh no. No, no, no. Please tell me I didn't fall asleep without finding out who she is.

I look around the bedroom I wake up in and recognize it as George's guest room from dozens of childhood sleepovers. I scramble to find anything that might indicate she left me some way to contact her. Did she put it on my phone? No. A note? No. Writing on my arm? There's nothing. All I have is my sandals, my keys, and my phone.

I lost her. I found my mate, and I fucking lost her.

Ah, fuck, there's no way George and Sally would let that happen. Those two are the sappiest lovebirds I've ever met. They wouldn't let a chance at love escape.

I scramble to get to the bedroom door, open it, and slide my way down George's apartment hallway until I get to the living room.

"George! Where are you? Come out here now before I have a goddamn aneurysm!" I shout when I find the living room empty. It may be a little dramatic, but it may not be. I could have a heart attack at this rate. All I know is my heart is screaming in my chest for *Sarah, Sarah, Sarah.* "Dear God I've lost the love of my life, have pity on me already!"

Several sets of feet come running down the hall, in the opposite direction from where I came earlier. I freeze in the dead center of the living room, under the brightness of the overhead light, in my red swim trunks. George, Sally, Sarah, and Teddy crowd together in the entryway, staring at me.

The stress from not knowing what happened to Sarah a moment ago and the embarrassment of having been found yelling about her meets in my belly and creates a reaction. I start to sweat, and my mouth goes dry. But that's not the worst part of it. I can feel them, the feathers, trying to poke through my skin.

Breathe, David. Calm down. She's here and safe. Everything will be fine.

I take deep, calming breaths and try to ignore the stares from the entryway. My stomach settles soon and the prickling feeling under my skin subsides. *Thank you.*

"David, what are you going on about?" Sally asks.

"Woke up and panicked. What happened? I remember being hit and this lovely woman introducing herself, and then nothing else."

Sarah brushes a strand of her ginger hair behind her ear and smiles when I call her lovely. She's put a white t-shirt and denim shorts over her swimsuit. The outfit looks classically sexy on her curves.

"You got knocked out and Sarah said you didn't want the hospital, so I brought you back here to watch over you. She and Teddy insisted on staying a little while to see if you woke up. Thankfully, you did. How are you feeling?" George asks.

"I feel quite alright, thank you." In fact, I feel fantastic. Other than the dizziness and nausea from the mate bond insisting I mate with Sarah *immediately*, of course.

"I'm so glad. I wanted to make sure you were alright. Not sure how I'll live without knowing what hobby you take up next now that you're done taking women's balls to the face." Sarah says with a short giggle before abruptly becoming quiet and stammering, "Not like, *balls*. I was joking about, you know how we were talking, and you said about the trying new things and…yeah."

Everyone laughs at Sarah's awkward attempt at conversation. She puts her face in her hands and shakes her head, laughing along with them. Good sense of humor. I like that.

"Well, whatever my new hobby is, hopefully I'm wearing a shirt and don't have sand in my hair while doing it.

Balls to the face or not," I run my fingers through my hair, grimacing as sand falls out. Yuck.

By this time, everyone has stopped lingering in the doorway and made their way to various seats around the living room. Sarah has chosen a seat next to the one I've sat down in. Teddy sits on my other side, staring me down hard the entire time.

"Well, what about the new aquarium that opened?" Sarah asks. "Have you been? Maybe you could get into studying fish. It looks really nice and big. I've been wanting to check it out but haven't had a chance."

"We could go together," I risk suggesting.

"I'd love that!" She claps her hands together and smiles, showing those dimples on her freckled cheeks.

"Oh God, Mom. You're just trying to get someone else to listen to you talk about fish. That's what this is about. I get it now," Teddy laughs.

Sarah frowns, crossing her arms under her chest.

"That's just a bonus." She nods in my direction. "I swear we'll have fun, and I won't talk about fish more than eighty percent of the time."

"That leaves her twenty percent to yap about aquatic mammals and birds, of course," Teddy snorts.

A special interest involving aquatic birds? Ah, *Sarah, Sarah, Sarah.*

Chapter Six

Sarah

"He's so cute. He's got this shiny black hair with threads of gray along the sides. Kind of a dad bod, chubby tummy but really nice forearms, you know? Gorgeous smile. Honestly, a bit of a nervous wreck but at the same time someone I desperately want to cuddle with."

"Seems like you just need someone to take care of now that Teddy's out of the house. You always did want a second child," Mira shakes her head at me on the screen.

"No, it's not like that. I mean, yes, I did enjoy having someone to fuss over, can't deny that." We both laugh. "But the moments he wasn't delirious from the head injury he was really funny, focused on what I was saying, nice to Teddy. Not to mention that he has actual friends of his own, is employed, and, again, cute. In this dating pool, I think that's a pretty good candidate for the first guy to take on a date in twenty years."

"Yeah, you're right. I'm just bitter because you didn't have to use a dating app to find him and some of us are stuck scrolling through disasters each weekend to find a potential suitor." Mira sighs. "Like, I saw four different guys on Matchr last night who said they were into ethical non-monogamy. But also said that they wanted to be the only dick in the relationship and that the women were only allowed to be with other women as long as he was involved. Oh, and even then, only skinny, cis, young women need apply."

My eyes practically roll out of my head.

"Oh, of course." My phone buzzes and I quickly pick it up to see who it is. *David.* "Oh my gosh, it's him."

"Open it! What does he want!"

"Hold on! Eee, I'm excited!"

I open the messages and my heart does little loops when I see his name. I'd left not long after we decided to go to the aquarium. I had things to do and work early, but we exchanged numbers to make plans.

David: Hello, Sarah. This is David. Though I suppose that'll show on your phone if this is the correct number. If it's not, then hello, stranger.

I laugh and continue reading.

David: Would Saturday at 5:00 be alright? I could pick you up, or we could meet there, whichever would make you feel more comfortable. That's of course if this is Sarah. If this is a stranger then I'm sorry but meeting there is the only option, I just don't feel comfortable picking up strangers. Apologies.

I laugh again and read the texts to Mira, who tries not to laugh but can't help herself.

"Okay. He's got a dumb sense of humor. He might win me over if he's good to you. What are you going to write back?"

I chew on my lip, a nervous habit, as I think about it, before replying.

Me: 5:00 sounds great. And yes, this is Sarah. As far as you know, anyway.

Me: I heard they have a really great exhibit on the Cambrian explosion with some really rare fossils set near their closest living modern relatives. Did you know that chordates emerged during the Cambrian era? That means we wouldn't have vertebrates, and therefore humans, without the Cambrian explosion. There were just a lot of really interesting creatures that came around then.

"Stop writing about whatever you're writing about," Mira says as she watches me type.

"The Cambrian explosion?"

"Especially that."

Me: Okay, enough about ancient creatures. I'll meet you there on Saturday. There's a big statue of a narwhal out front we can meet in front of. See you then!

Almost immediately I break out into a huge grin as the three dots show up on my screen. He's writing back!

"He's writing! Ah! I love a fast response."

"I know you do. You're probably the most impatient person I've ever met."

David: Five it is then, next to the narwhal. I would avoid the front of any narwhal if I were you.

Me: You have a point.

David: So does the narwhal.

Later, when I show Teddy the texts, he can't help but crack a grin at the narwhal comment. I really don't want to date anyone my son doesn't approve of, so that smile means a lot to me. People might think it's unhealthy to care what my adult son thinks of someone I'm dating, but I don't. He's been my whole life for so long. And I'm not going to just jump into something with someone he doesn't like. No way.

"He's a dork, Mom. But so are you." Teddy ruffles my hair as he passes by me on the way out the door. "Sorry, I can't stay long, school, then work. Love you!"

"Love ya too, buddy!"

Waving my son out the door, I think again for the millionth time what it would be like to have another kid. I like being a mom. My first time around was rough at first, being so young. But I toughed it out, me and my little guy against the world, and we made it. What would it be like now that I had experience? What would it be like with a second parent to help out?

Eh, that's just a dream. I've already had my chance. Now is just the time for fun. Like hanging out at aquariums.

When Saturday rolls around, I'm in a total panic, of course. The first date in *twenty years* is kind of a big deal, after all. Mira calms me down, though, and helps me decide what to wear. A white blouse, some dark jeans, and gold sandals. It's very basic and very millennial. But that's fitting, considering I'm a pretty basic millennial and all. I do my makeup and hair very simply, nervously pee about fifty times, and then leave way too early for the museum.

I get there at 4:40, expecting to stand there and play around on my phone for twenty minutes. My phone stays in my purse, however.

"David? You're early!"

He's standing next to the narwhal statue, just like he said he'd be. And wow, he's gorgeous.

His black and gray hair is neatly combed to look smooth and shiny. He's wearing a black button-up shirt, with the sleeves rolled up to expose his forearms. *Slutty*. His gray pants show off his little bubble butt wonderfully. But his bright smile and warm, dark eyes are the best part.

"Yes, sorry. Was so worried about being late I ended up on the other side of time, I guess. But you're here too. More time together can't be a bad thing, right?"

"I suppose you're right. And more time with the isopods. They have a giant isopod on display here. Very few places in the country have one! They're such interesting creatures. They're related to little roly-poly bugs, which are crustaceans, not insects by the way, but they're so much bigger. And–"

David holds out his elbow.

"Perhaps we should go in and see them. You can tell me more about them on the way," he says.

Blushing, I take his arm, and we walk toward the entrance.

"Sorry, I get excited and ramble on."

"Please don't be sorry. I was enjoying listening to you. Just assumed you'd like to see the exhibit as well. Now, are sow bugs really crustaceans? That can't be true, can it?"

"Oh, but it is!"

As we enter the aquarium, I can see in his mannerisms David is genuinely paying attention to what I'm saying. That he doesn't think I'm stupid for being so excited. I could just about swoon. Instead, I point to the start of the exhibits.

"Anemone. Let's go!"

Chapter Seven
David

S he sure does love aquatic life. Especially talking about it. It's a good thing I like listening to her.

It's getting harder and harder to focus on anything but her with each passing moment. The mate bond is getting quite aggressive about pushing me toward her. As if I am not already very aware of her existence. I've had a hard time keeping my stress reactions in check and have had to do some serious meditation to control myself.

My penguin features were popping out wildly all morning. Even last night, due to nervousness. My feet were webbed when I woke up, for fuck's sake. I was pulling feathers out of my hair until almost three o'clock. For two hours, I had a left flipper instead of a hand. But now I've got it all together, thank God. Except, I can't stop thinking about the rocks.

My kind gifts rocks to our mates. It's a leftover bit of evolution from before we separated from the penguin ancestors, I assume. We gift them a lot of rocks. Pretty rocks.

It's a biological urge. And it's goddamn overwhelming right now.

So, while I should be enjoying this date with a beautiful woman, I'm instead fighting off feather growth, resisting the urge to go outside and find some rocks, trying not to stare at her cleavage, and repeating *Sarah, Sarah, Sarah* over and over in my head. It's a fucking mess.

"Oh look, penguins!"

I snap out of my haze and follow Sarah's pointing finger. There is indeed an exhibit of penguins. Adélie penguins. The bastards.

"Those sons of bitches," I spit out. "Worst of the worst. The women aren't so bad, but the men...the men you've got to stay away from."

Sarah blinks at me silently a few times. She looks back and forth between the penguins and me.

"You are talking about those little penguins, right?"

Squinting my eyes at the hell beasts to make sure they're locked up tight, I take Sarah's arm again and walk away from the exhibit.

"Let's move along. The seals are up next. At least everyone knows they're predators."

"Uh, okay."

We walk toward the aquatic mammal area but in the center of the aquarium is a food court and gift shop. We pass by the food, and I wonder if she's hungry.

"Would you like to stop and get something to eat or drink?"

"I'm fine unless you want something. I do want to check out the gift shop though. Get something for Teddy."

"Sure." I smile at her, still buying little treats for her grown-up boy.

We get to the gift shop and look at all the science-themed gifts. Bumper stickers, stuffed animals, t-shirts. But then I feel a pull in my stomach. I follow the tug and it leads me to an area of the store with a big sign that says, "Fill a bag, $10."

Oh no. I can feel my pupils grow huge. My feathers scratch barely below the surface of my skin. The impulse is too strong. I let out a great, resigned sigh and prepare for awkwardness and spending great multiples of ten dollars.

Taking several little mesh bags and a wicker basket, I head to the first section of the display and start grabbing. *Agates. Quartz. Fluorite. Obsidian. Amethyst.* The list goes on. What are meant to be rocks kids can buy to start a rock collection or something of the sort, will now be an embarrassing gift to Sarah.

Resigned to my fate, I continue to fill up bags with lovely stones. Sarah comes over with a curious look on her face.

"What's going on there?"

"I, uh, think stones are great. Really great. Just, the best." Pretty hard to play up the enthusiasm for a mesh bag full of granite, but I'm doing my best.

"Oh, yes, there are so many lovely ones. You sure are getting a lot of them."

"Yes. I need a lot of them." I attempt to smile as the need to continue acquiring the stones is battering at my insides.

"Okay! I'm going to go buy this shirt for Teddy. It says 'I'd Rather Be a Frog' in a really beautiful art nouveau design. It's so strange. He'll love it."

She wanders away toward the checkout, and I let out a relieved breath as I hurry to scoop up as many rocks as I can.

An employee notices the panicked look on my face as the second wicker basket full of little mesh bags nearly slips from my arms.

"Hello, sir. Can I help you?" the woman asks.

I'm about to make up some sort of excuse when I sense it. This woman is like me. Well, sort of. I don't think she's of penguin lineage. She doesn't smell right. But I can tell she's something.

"It's uh, it's an unfortunately timed mate bond urge. Can't seem to stop myself from gathering up the rocks." I speak quietly enough for the people around us not to hear but the employee hears well enough. Our kind tend to have better hearing than most.

She nods in understanding and holds one finger up to indicate I should hold on before walking away. When she returns a moment later, she's got a cart with a large crate on it.

"Put them all in here and I'll ring you up. I'll have it delivered to you. There's no way you'll be able to carry them all through the aquarium. Will that be alright?"

I check with my inner animal. I don't like that I won't be giving them to her straight away, but knowing I'll own them and have them all in my home to give her privately is more desirable than trying to do something in public, anyway. Alright, I'll push down the impatience and have them delivered. Delivered immediately, of course.

"That would be perfect. Thank you for understanding."

"Not a problem. You're luckier than I was anyway. I'm a porcupine, and so is my mate. He fully succumbed to his mating urge in public, unfortunately. He spent the first year of our relationship in prison." She loads the rocks into the crate while my eyebrows raise in surprise.

"Prison? What kind of mating ritual could that be?"

She sighs, pinches the bridge of her nose, and huffs a soft laugh.

"He took off his pants in the mall and pissed all over me."

I drop my wicker basket of rocks onto the table. She continues.

"He couldn't control it. Was like a total zombie. My point is your rocks aren't so bad. You could be a porcupine. Or worse...an angler fish."

We both shudder then. My rocks really aren't so bad.

Chapter Eight
Sarah

The rest of the aquarium visit is delightful. He's a total sweetheart. Listens to me babble on without looking bored or trying to change the subject. Asks me about myself and my interests. And the things he tells me about himself are great. Like he loves swimming, sushi, and romantic movies. He cares a lot about animals. Above all, family is really important to him. I really like that.

When the date is over, I have a hard time saying goodbye. I want him to ask me over to his place or something, but instead, he's a perfect gentleman and asks if I'd like to get together again *soon*. Argh. I swiftly agree and we've made a date for next Friday night. It feels like the next century it's so far away, ugh.

During the week we text constantly. Mira tells me that means he's got it bad for me. Like, he doesn't just text one-word responses, he actually replies thoughtfully. We have real conversations. As the week approaches Friday, things start to get a little bit steamy.

David: Still up for tomorrow night? I'll pick you up at seven, your place, dinner at Chico's.

Me: For the twentieth time, yes. I haven't changed my mind.

David: Sorry. Still finding it hard to believe such a lovely woman is going out with me twice. The aquarium could have been some sort of accident but twice is intentional.

Me: Oh, stop. I'm not that great, lol.

David: Don't put yourself down. I bet you look gorgeous even now in the middle of a work night, while the rest of us look like slobs in our pajamas.

I chew on my lip before deciding to send him a picture of myself. I'm wearing a tank top without a bra, my hair up in a messy bun. I pull my hair out of the bun and give it a good shake. It looks wild and tangled, believable as bedtime hair, but a bit full and sexy as well. My tits are on the saggy end of life, so I pose with my arm under them to give them a bit of a boost and their best shot at a nice photograph. I let the strap on my tank fall off my shoulder and my mouth pop open slightly. Now there's a nice and smutty pose. I snap the photo and hit send, nerves swirling around in my stomach as I wait for a reply to my first dating selfie.

David: Christ, Sarah. Are you trying to kill me? You're a heartstopper if there ever was one.

Me: Oh. Jeez. You've got me blushing now.

David: You've got me more than blushing. I'll not say more than that.

Me: You could...

David: Or I could talk to you in person tomorrow, Sarah...I think I'd like that better.

Me: I think I might like that too. We'll see.

My entire body tingles and my heart races as I think of the possibilities. Is he going to whisper naughty things to me? Are we going to do naughty things? I can't wait!

The next day I put on a little green dress, high heels, and lacy underwear. The restaurant is supposed to be nice, so I want to look decent, but I also want to look a little bit like I'm trying too hard to get him into bed. Because I am. Truth in advertising and all that. It's been twenty years and for the first time I really, really want someone. So I'm gonna go for it.

At exactly seven, he pulls up in his black sedan. It's a nice car. He's got a good job as a hydrologist that supports him well. He says he enjoys it too, and that he has pretty good job security where he is.

As I climb into the car, I can see a blush wash over his cheeks when he notices me watching him look at my bare legs. I can't help but giggle as I put the seatbelt on. He clears his throat and pulls away from the curb.

"You look lovely tonight, Sarah."

"Thank you. I'm looking forward to our dinner."

"Me too."

The rest of our drive is polite conversation, but there is a definite tension between us. As if something is waiting to snap. We manage to make it to the restaurant anyway.

We're seated and given our drinks. Neither of us has wine tonight. It turns out, neither of us is big on alcohol except for the occasional beach beer, on his part. We order our food, both of us getting fish dishes, and settle in to wait.

"You know, it's strange because we've just met, but I really like you, Sarah. I can already tell how wonderful you are," he says, head laid on the palm of his hand, a dreamy look to his eyes.

"I like you too. David. So, I'm strange too, I guess."

"Strange? No. Intelligent, sweet, kind, fun to be around? Yes." He pauses with his water lifted part of the way to his mouth with a playful glint in his eyes. "Well, maybe the excessive amount of knowledge you have involving crustaceans for someone who isn't employed in any field involving them is a little odd, but I find it charming."

"Hey, maybe someday I'll be doing pedicures, and someone will have a decapod emergency. You never know."

I take a drink of my own water, trying to stifle a giggle as I do.

"That's true." David nods solemnly. "You never know when someone's crab needs its toenails painted."

I'm almost spitting my water out laughing as the waiter brings our dishes to the table. The food looks wonderful and tastes even better. David tells me about his job. It's important work that he doesn't find exactly exciting, but he's happy to be doing, nonetheless. I tell him more about my job doing pedicures, which can get weird sometimes, but most days is pretty dull. We're almost done eating when he pauses what he's saying with a funny look on his face and shakes his head.

"Sarah, I'm sorry but I just can't get over how beautiful you look. That color green is perfect for you. A lovely forest color. Though, I'm sure you'd look good in any color, of course."

"Oh yeah? What other colors should I wear?" Maybe this will be a hint to him that I want another date.

"Ah, perhaps a nice berry color. A deep magenta sort, almost purple. Something like that. Really though, anything would look good." He shrugs.

I just barely stop myself from chewing on my lip. *Should I go for it?* I drum my fingers on the table a couple of times. *Fuck it.*

"A berry color, huh?" My voice has taken on a huskier-than-usual tone. "I am wearing that. Would you like to see?"

David looks confused for a second before his face smooths out, his eyes sliding from my face to the front of my dress as he nods his affirmation. I look around quickly to make sure no one is paying attention before sliding the thick strap of my dress down, revealing the berry-colored strap of the lacy bra I'm wearing underneath. I quickly cover back up before anyone notices, my cheeks burning red. David swallows, clears his throat.

"A lovely color indeed. Of course, it would be easier to judge if I could see more of the set, but I'm sure it's fine."

"Oh, I don't want you to have any lingering doubts. Maybe we should go to your house and I can show you both pieces. Then you can tell me if it's as nice as you were thinking it would be."

Oh boy. Here we go.

"I think that's a fantastic idea."

The light seems to shine strangely on the side of David's neck for a moment, making it appear black. *No.* It *is* black. My head tilts to the side as I point to the shiny area that seems to have come out of nowhere.

"David, you have something on your right there."

He slaps at the side of his neck, his eyes growing wide as he feels what's there. Quickly he hustles to the men's room, hand still over the patch on his neck.

In a moment he returns, back to normal.

"That was odd," he says as he shakes his head. "There were feathers on my neck. Don't know where they came from. One of these people's fancy outfits perhaps? Strange though."

"Huh. Weird." I shrug it off. Not letting that get in the way of my goal. "So, are we staying for dessert or do you think we're ready to go?"

I smooth my hair over one side of my neck, letting my bare shoulder bring back the moment before the feather incident. His half-lidded expression tells me I've succeeded in my attempt.

"I'm quite ready to go if you are of course."

"I'm very, very ready."

David signals to the waiter that we'd like our check. A few minutes later, we're out the door.

Chapter Nine
David

Oh shit. I can't bring her back to the apartment. Fucking Christ David. Stop yourself. What are you doing?

No, she's my mate. I've got to bring her back home. She's ready to breed. I can taste her in the air. Sarah, Sarah, Sarah.

She can't come back, not with the state of the place. Not with all of the–

"David, are you okay?" Sarah interrupts my thoughts.

"Yeah, I'm fine. Just distracted, sorry. It's close, we'll be there in a minute."

She's going to think I'm fucking insane. I can't sleep with her before telling her I'm a gentoo, it's just not right. But I didn't want her to find out like this. I'll stop and turn around, take her home. Make some excuse why she can't come in.

I can't though. The inside of me is too strong. It's like the woman at the aquarium was saying about her piss mate. I'm like a zombie to my animal half.

Take her inside and breed her. Mate now.

Shut up. I'm going as fast as I can.

Sarah, Sar–

"David, you ran a red light!" Sarah gasps.

"Oh God, I'm sorry. I guess, uh, I'm nervous. That must be it."

"Please don't be." She sets her soft hand on mine. "Or at the very least don't kill us."

"I promise I'll try at least one of those."

She groans at my bad joke but doesn't have to deal with my terrible sense of humor in the car too much longer since we arrive at my house just then. I pull into the driveway and take a deep breath, trying not to scratch at the feathers I can feel poking through the skin on my thighs.

All the nerves are making it impossible to hold back the penguin features. If I'm not careful, I'm going to end up with a goddamn cloaca before the night is over. No one wants that.

Go go go! Mate! Inside! Move!

Alright! I'm going!

The push to take her inside is so strong it's painful. I can't resist.

"Here we are. My little nest." I take her hand and lead her to the front door. After I unlock it I stand there for a moment, desperately trying to turn away.

GO NOW! INSIDE!

With a resigned sigh, I open the door and walk her inside. The room is dim when I close the door behind us, and when I turn the light on it's still pretty dim.

Because the lamps are blocked.

By stacks of stones.

In fact, everything is blocked by stacks of stones. There are rocks everywhere, big and small, they have nothing in common except they all look at least a little pretty.

If I'm making her a nest, it's got to be pretty.

"Uh...what an interesting room," Sarah says as she looks around, not moving from in front of the door. "Do you have furniture?"

"Yes. It's in the other rooms. This happens to be the largest room and I thought it would be best suited for the nest." I clear my throat and cross my arms over my chest. The feathers are popping up on my back now. I can feel them.

"The nest? What does that mean?"

I nervously shift from foot to foot. Wasn't prepared to explain this all to her so soon. Then again, I did say I wanted a relationship like my Mom and Dad had. They knew right away.

"Do you know anything about gentoo penguins?" I ask.

"A little, but I'm not as knowledgeable about aquatic birds as I could be."

"Alright. Well. Gentoo penguins, uh, they're a monogamous bird and when they couple up they use rocks to impress their mate and to make a nest to lay their eggs."

"And gentoo penguins have to do with you making a big old rock nest in your human house why exactly?" she asks, and suddenly seems closer to the door than before.

"There's another fact about them, well their ancestors. At one point in evolution, they split off and somehow became entangled with humans. Judging by other similar beings it looks to have been magic, probably. But however it happened, a gentoo-human race was created. We stayed isolated, scattered about in the Falkland Islands. But we've spread out. And here I am." I laugh nervously and open my arms wide.

"Okay. I should have known this was too good to be true. Meeting the perfect guy on the first try after twenty years? Yeah, right. Of course he'd be a nut job." She turns the door handle. "Bye."

"No, please, I can prove it. Please don't go. Sarah."

Thankfully, she forgot to turn the lock before the handle, so it gives me a moment to rush to hold the door. She tries to push past me, her face turning angry and frightened, much to my dismay.

"Sarah, please."

Suddenly, she gasps, stumbling backward.

"Feathers. All over. What the fuck?"

I feel them then. On my neck, face, hands. Black and white feathers.

"I told you I was telling the truth. Will you please talk to me? Just talk?"

Sarah nods silently, continuing to look me over. I gesture toward the kitchen and we follow a path through the rocks to get there. It's a much more normal space in the kitchen, which is helpful. Though, I look more out of place here like this. I pull out a chair at the kitchen table for Sarah to sit, and we both take our seats across from one another.

"Alright. As you can see, I can transform. This is just a partial transformation. When I get nervous or upset my penguin features start to emerge. I have to hold them back and normally I'm good at that. This time, however, things are different because my hormones are out of control around you. I've pretty much got an animal in my head twenty-four hours a day screaming at me to bring you home to my nest and make you my mate. I've been keeping it under control by building said nest. It's done being controlled now, though, I guess." I fold my hands in my lap and stare down at the chipped edge of the wood table. This is all insane to explain to anyone who's not our kind. She's going to run away screaming.

Fuck.

"Do you think the magic is part of nature or do you think it's something separate? And if it's something separate then what exactly is it? Are there other kinds of animal people and are they made from magic-infused evolution too? Are there any creatures human people know about that are made from magic but we don't know it? Oh! Are there any animal hybrid people that I would know about, like historically well-known people or something? Are there other types of magical occurrences?"

Sarah looks at me, waiting for answers to her questions, but I sit in shocked silence instead. She didn't run away! She's still sitting there, looking as beautiful as ever.

"David?"

"Sorry. That's a lot of information to share. We have whole classes for some of that. But for some easy stuff, yes there are other animal people. George, my friend you met, was a penguin as well, for example."

"Really? Interesting. Could there be any type of animal people? Even crustacean people?" She cocks her head to the side and waits for my response.

"I suppose it's possible, though I've never met anyone. I would hope you wouldn't go looking for a crustacean mate when you have a very enthusiastic avian contender right here. Can't stop you, of course. Just really hopeful."

Sarah wrinkles her nose in disgust.

"There's nothing sexy to me about a hard exoskeleton and segmented legs, David."

"I'm not sure there's anything sexy about feathers and flippers to you either," I say with a cringe.

"What is sexy is how well we get along. How considerate you are of my feelings."

I hold my breath as she leans over the table, reaches out her hand, and strokes the very tips of two fingers down my cheek.

"Your feathers are so smooth. I'm not really sure what I expected them to feel like. I like it though."

She runs both hands down my cheeks, down the sides of my neck. I close my eyes, breathe in the scent of her, and let myself enjoy this moment before she inevitably gains her sanity and leaves.

No! No leaving! Take her! I must take my mate. Right here.

Ah, fuck. That's not how that works. You can't just toss a woman over the table and–

Do it.

"I think I'm losing control, Sarah," I grit out between my teeth. "The same animal that's forcing its way out of me is trying to force itself into you, if you get my drift. You should go and we can talk when I can get myself together again."

"What happens if I don't go?" Sarah asks as she gets up from her seat, walks around the table, and perches on the side of it next to me. "What will happen to me?"

"Sarah, this isn't a good idea." I kick off my shoes as the bones begin to break in my feet. Fuck, I hate having the penguin feet. Makes for awkward walking.

"Why? We were planning on coming back here for...*that* anyway, weren't we? Now you just look a little different. It's just feathers, right?" Sarah kicks off her heels, her little, magenta-painted toenails wiggling adorably.

JUST FUCK HER. SARAHSARAHSARAHSARAH-SARAH

I clutch my hair, trying to get the voice in my head to quiet down. At least let me have a fucking conversation.

"Things are different now because you have about thirty seconds before I treat you like an animal and not the lovely, sweet, woman you are." I clutch at my lower back as my spine stretches, curving out into a short tail. "Go."

Sarah stands up, reaches behind herself, and unzips her dress. The lovely green fabric falls to the floor in a puddle around her bare feet. Before me, she stands in her berry-colored lingerie, which is much lacier and covers much less than I expected. No real thoughts pass through my head; every space is taken by her.

When the scent of her, the real hidden scent of her, hits me finally, everything shatters. I'm up and out of the chair in a flash.

Take her.

I do. She gasps as I force her over the table, my body on top of her. I grind my hard cock into her ass as I take a great inhale of her scent along the side of her neck. I stop at her ear and huff a laugh.

"Mind if I take you on the stones actually? I put a lot of work into it and it's sort of tradition."

There's a pause before Sarah breaks out into giggles. I want to be offended but I can't help laughing along with her. Yes, my animal is screaming and flapping and squawking but I just can't do it. I want to take my time with her. Save the rough and wild for another day. This is our first mating.

It's also the first time I have sex at all, but I'm not going to mention that.

Chapter Ten
Sarah

David picks me up and carries me back to the living room where there's a flattened area in the rocks, blankets on top of them, and lays me down. I was a little afraid when he bent me over in the kitchen, I'll admit it. It seemed like it would be fun, the way he was talking about being all animalistic, but when it started, I panicked. It's been so long for me. I don't want my first time back at it to be a quick fuck. All I've ever really had was quickies. I was a teen the only times I've done it before. And teen boys aren't exactly known for being skilled in the bedroom. So, when David stopped and said we were going to go to the living room, I felt much, much better.

"You alright?" he asks, kneeling beside me, stroking my hair.

It's so strange. He's covered in feathers. If anyone would have asked me if I thought it attractive, I would have laughed at them. But seeing it on him is different. It's beautiful. I have a feeling in my belly I wouldn't think that about anyone else, though. Just David.

"Yeah, I'm fine." I stroke his smooth cheek. It's such an interesting feeling, I can't seem to stop myself. "Are you feathered all over under those clothes?"

Hint hint.

"Mostly. Not, uh, in some more sensitive areas." He begins to unbutton his shirt, pauses. "It's alright?"

"David, please. Somewhere between this and the table. That's the level of action we should be at. Okay?" I sit up and start to unbutton his shirt for him. "It's been a while for me, and I want to take our time. But I also want you very badly, so please don't be shy or worried."

"Got it." His voice is rough and deep as he compliments me, "God, you're beautiful. Even your hands are perfect."

I undo his belt buckle, and the button of his pants, teasingly pausing at the top of his zipper.

"You only like my hands because they're undressing you."

"That certainly helps. I'd love them even if they were covering me in duct tape though."

"Duct tape? Come on now, we'll save the kinky stuff for another time."

"Oh lord no, please, the feathers. Duct tape and feathers don't mix." He shudders and I can't help but laugh. But then I slowly start to unzip his pants, and no one is laughing.

David lies back as I tug off his pants and black boxer briefs. True to his word he's mostly covered in black and white feathers, except for his cock and balls. It's sort of strange looking at first but it doesn't take long to get used to it, especially when I start to touch him. His enthusiastic reaction is so attractive I can't be anything but attracted in return.

"Fuck, Sarah, I think I like your hands even more now."

Okay, I'm stroking his cock before I even kiss him. I think I'm doing this wrong. Back up.

"Can I kiss you?" With way more nervousness than I should be showing at this point.

"Please do, Sarah," he replies as he sits up, places his hands on the side of my face, then his lips on mine.

It's a perfect first kiss. Even though I still have my hand on his cock, I realize. Well, that doesn't matter, I guess. His mouth is perfect, anyway. His lips are soft. He takes control of the kiss and he's just a little rough, but not brutish. It's not sloppy, but it's a little wet. Basically, it's passionate.

I fucking love it.

I grab at the back of his hair and force the kiss deeper, harder. He groans and I realize I'm stroking him harder, faster as the kiss goes on. His breathing stutters. My hand is wet. The kiss stops.

"Shit. Sorry," David forces out, "Didn't see it coming until I was, uh, coming."

He leans back, grabs one of the small blankets at the side of the flattened area, and wipes my hand.

"It's okay. I mean, that's kind of what happens," I say with a giggle. "What else would we expect?"

"Perhaps that I would be able to withstand touch longer than two minutes."

"It was less than two minutes for sure." I grin.

"Thank you for the correction."

"You're welcome." I push his chest until he's lying down, then I lay next to him with my head on his chest. He seems surprised but wraps his arm around me. "That was a good thing anyway. Got the first one out of the way. Now the second one you'll last longer. That's how it works, right?"

"Generally, yeah." He pauses before half turning to look at me. "So, you still want to be with me tonight?"

"Uh, yeah. I didn't come all this way over here for nothing." I raise an eyebrow.

"Thank the lord."

David rolls on top of me, kissing me hard. I wrap my legs around his waist, my arms around his neck. We kiss for several long minutes before he slides his hands behind us and unclasps my bra. We pull apart so he can take it off of me. Somewhere in the back of my mind is a little voice telling me I should be embarrassed by not being young and perky anymore, but I squash that voice. I still have tits and they're mine and he'll like them, or he won't.

And oh boy, does he. His pupils get huge when he sees me fully topless. He stares for so long that I worry I'm going to have to slap him back into reality before he speaks.

"How do you just keep getting better and better? You're going to kill me," he rasps out before he dips down and licks my hard nipple.

He licks and sucks on them with great enthusiasm. Strokes and gently squeezes my breasts, and grinds his now-hard again cock between my legs. I moan at the feeling, never knowing my nipples would be this sensitive. No one had ever paid attention to them like this before. It feels so good, but what feels even better is what he's doing with his right hand now.

He's slipped his hand inside my panties and slid his fingers through my wetness, of which there is plenty. His fingertips gently rub my clit in soft circles.

I think I'm going to die. It feels too good. His mouth. His hand. It's so much.

"Oh fuck, David. So good. I'm gonna–"

And then I'm squeezing my thighs around him and gritting my teeth, trying not to scream. Maybe at some point, I'll make a lot of noise when I come, but I'm still a little shy. Can't be perfect, I guess. Either way, it feels fucking fantastic.

"There we go. That's my girl," David smiles against my chest as I come down from my orgasm.

"That was...that was..."

"That was less than two minutes," David winks.

"I want to throw something at you, but my body is too weak right now," I pant out.

"That's the plan. Weaken you so I can ravish you. It's genius, really."

"Foolish man. 'Tis I that will ravish you." I hold up a finger. "Just gimme a sec to get my legs working again."

David lurches forward and grabs hold of me, wrapping his arms around me, and caging me in with his legs. He gives me a heated, half-lidded look. He looks as if he's about to make a smart-ass reply, but instead, he shakes his head and then kisses me.

Soon enough, his hands slide down my waist. When they reach my hips, he slips his fingers into the waist of my lacy panties and slides them down, breaking our kiss as he goes. He pulls them off of my feet, then places soft kisses up my ankle, my calf, my thigh. My heart races as he reaches the place where my thighs end and he looks up at me, a devious grin in his eyes. I both want him to do what I think he's going to do and don't want him to at the same time. Because I want to get to the next part. Badly. So, so badly.

"David," I begin.

"Yes?" he answers, before licking a firm line up my center, ending with deep pressure on my already sensitive clit.

My eyes roll back as I moan and grab at his hair, pulling him back.

"Fuck that feels good. But not now. Now I want you."

"What exactly is it you want, Sarah?" he asks with a mischievous glint in his eyes.

"You, David. Now. Inside me. I want–" Okay, I can do this, I can talk dirty in person. Come on, Sarah, you got this. "I want your cock inside me. Please fuck me."

David breathes out, his eyes closed and a smile on his face. He crawls up slowly.

"You want my cock in this pretty little cunt of yours, Sarah? Stretch you out and fill you up? I want to feel every part of you, Sarah. Go to your deepest spaces. I want to get inside you and not come out until you're wrecked for anyone but me. You're my fucking mate. Whatever you want, I'll give you. No matter what. If you want me to fuck you, then you're going to get one hell of a fuck. Spread your legs wide for me and don't be shy. I want to see my treasure."

I about die from the speech but do as he says and spread my legs apart. He backs up onto his knees and sits for a long moment, just staring between my legs, stroking his cock. I feel completely exposed and vulnerable, but when I see how fast he's breathing, I feel pretty hot, too. Tentatively, I reach down and run a finger along the center of my pussy. He groans in delight. I smirk and do it again.

"I think I've been officially tortured enough." He fits himself into position.

My heart races. This is it. Twenty years. The head of his cock presses against my incredibly wet opening. My mouth drops open, going dry in nervousness. We look into one another's eyes as he pushes in.

It's slow, and it's a tight fit at first. He's gentle and patient. It doesn't hurt or anything, it's not like that. Just extra pressure. It actually feels nice. Really nice. I hold him against me and lift my hips to meet his until we're firmly fitted together. We fit perfectly. My breath comes out in shaky *ohs* as we begin to move together, working faster and faster.

I push his shoulders until he rolls over, and I'm on top, working my hips much better than I thought I could. Thank you dance classes that Mira made me take.. David places a thumb on my clit and circles it as I ride, and it isn't too long before I'm coming hard around his cock. As soon as I'm mostly down from my orgasm, David lifts me off him and flips me over, setting me down on all fours.

"Now I claim my mate," he growls out. And it's a real growl. Who knew penguins growled? "I'm going to breed this sweet cunt. No more of this human romance nonsense."

"Wait what?" My foggy post-orgasm brain catches his words but doesn't really process them before his cock slams into me and I'm moaning again.

Chapter Eleven
David

Well, I managed to satisfy the animal side for the most part, but now it's had enough. Couldn't just shut up. Thankfully, I think Sarah was well fucked enough she didn't comprehend the lunacy I was spouting. *"Human nonsense,"* come on now!

I don't have much time to wallow in self-pity, however, when my cock is back inside her. Nothing in the world feels better than this. She's so fucking slippery after coming. Holy shit. I didn't know it would be like that. I'm learning so many new things today.

"Yes, David. Oh, fuck me. Your cock feels so good," Sarah says, and her voice sounds like a whine, like she's begging. *Fucking hell, that's hot.*

"This cock is for you, Sarah. It better feel good. It's all yours. Take it. Take this cock in your hungry pussy."

"Yes, give it to me. Fuck," she clenches around me, and I know it'll be easy to make her come again. I lean my weight on one hand and rub her clit with the other until she's gripping my dick hard with her cunt and shouting, "David! Fuck!"

I think I like the shouting. Didn't know she had it in her. Actually, I *know* I like the shouting because I tense up and start to get that feeling in my legs and gut that lets me know it's about that time.

"Oh, fuck." My tail stiffens. "Oh, Sarah."

And then I'm coming inside her. Filling her up with my hot cum. Through my haze, I hear her moan along with me as we both relax our bodies to the floor. I stay inside her, laying on top, careful not to crush her, until I grow soft. I roll us over until we're on our sides and I hold her tight against my chest.

My animal is quiet for now. Thank fuck.

"You alright?" I ask.

"Mmm, very."

The bones in my feet crack and I feel them returning to their human shape. My feathers retreat. My tail is the last stubborn bit to go, but eventually it does.

"Hey, you," Sarah says as she turns around to face me, pressing our bodies front to front. My cock twitches at the feeling of her breasts pressed against me, but I tell it to sit the fuck down.

"Hey. Hope you still like me without the feathers."

"You're alright," she laughs as she strokes my cheek. "Different texture but I still like it."

She kisses me, soft and sweet, then presses her face against my chest.

"Will the feathery stuff happen all the time?"

"No. I was...overcome with my instincts. It was forced out of me. Normally it only happens if I will it to, or if I'm under great stress."

"I might miss the tail."

"We'll see if we can't get it to make an occasional appearance."

Chapter Twelve

Sarah

"Mira, I don't feel so good."

I sit in front of the camera as we do our normal chatting routine. It's been a few days since my first date with David. We've seen each other every night since. I can't help it. It's like I'm drawn to his side. But this morning by the time I got home I felt like I was going to barf. And now I think I really might.

"Don't tell me you aren't using birth control," she raises a brow.

"Of course I am. You think I didn't learn before?" I roll my eyes. "I must just be sick."

"Condom too?"

"Well..." I find it impossible to look her in the eyes.

"Sarah!"

"I know! It was the heat of the moment! And then a lot of moments. I'm dumb, I know. But either way, I'm not pregnant. Just sick."

"Be smart, Sarah."

"I–"

I throw up.

And the next morning. And afternoon.

Soon, I start getting some additional suspicious symptoms like fatigue and sensitive breasts. It's way too soon to be showing symptoms like that if it was pregnancy, though. So, I go to the doctor to get checked out for illness. Of course, the first thing they check for is pregnancy. And it comes back a big, fat, positive.

Fuck.

I go home and cry. Then I cry some more. What's he going to say? What am I going to do?

I curl up on the sofa and take a long nap. When I wake up, I open my laptop and do a lot of penguin research. Then I call David and ask to meet him at his house.

"Hey. How are you, darling?" he asks as I step inside. I know I look like shit, but I also know he'd never say that. He probably would never even think that.

"Did you know that gentoo penguins actually give *each other* rocks when they want to mate? It's not just one giving to the other," I say.

"Well, yes. But you're a human so–"

"I was just thinking that tradition is tradition, ya know?" I pull a pretty piece of quartz I found in my garden out of my pocket and hand it to David. "If we maybe become a family someday, we should have traditions."

David holds the quartz in his hands as if it's incredibly delicate. The edges of his eyes glisten.

"If maybe," he says softly.

"David, what if, um, that family thing started a little sooner than expected? Maybe a lot sooner, actually." My stomach turns and I sway on my feet, trying not to tip over from the nausea.

"Are you– You're not saying–"

"Yeah, I am. I mean, it's still *really* early so who knows what could happen, but the doctor says I'm pregnant. I used birth control, I swear, so I have no idea how–"

"Holy shit, we're gonna be parents. I can't believe it. This is amazing. This is the best day of my life!" David takes my face in his hands and plants a kiss on my lips. "You're going to lay the best eggs; I just know it."

I shake my head, stunned by his reaction for several reasons, the biggest one being the egg thing.

"Well, I'm not sure what they taught you in the Falklands, honey, but people don't lay eggs."

"Oh. About that. You will." He kisses me on the cheek before walking away to start rearranging some rocks. "Won't be long either, so we better start preparing the nest."

"That's not funny, David. Don't joke with a pregnant lady like that. I'm already emotional as it is."

"Sarah, I'm not joking." He stops what he's doing and returns to take my hands. He guides me to sit down. "You're gonna lay an egg, probably two, in about 30 days. The two of us will be compelled to share the duty of keeping them warm by sitting on them for another 30-40 days. Then they hatch. Voila, baby."

We sit in silence for a long time. A million things run through my mind. *How am I going to explain this to Teddy?*

"I'm sorry I didn't tell you, Sarah. I didn't think it would happen so soon. I suppose, I should have realized when my animal immediately shut up that the deed was done but I didn't expect to get a woman pregnant the first time I ever had sex. What kind of luck is that?" He pinches the bridge of his nose while I blink at him.

"What do you mean the first time?"

"Ah. Well. I didn't plan on having sex unless I met my mate, and was never particularly interested. Of course, as soon as I met you, I read about every guide I could find on sex. They mostly just said when in doubt try to locate the clitoris. Seemed to work out."

"Yeah, it did, but still. I would have liked to have known."

"It would only have made things awkward. We already had a little bit of trouble with the whole me being a penguin thing. Didn't want to make it worse."

"I guess. Anyway, I have about a month before I lay an egg. Maybe two eggs." I stare ahead of me in disbelief.

"Probably two."

I laugh. Keep laughing. Pretty soon I'm laughing uncontrollably. *I'm laying eggs. Penguin eggs. That'll hatch into babies.*

"You sure you're alright, darling?" David wraps his arms around me, and my laughs turn to tears, then to sniffles, and then I quiet.

We spend the night mostly quiet, laying together, him comforting me and reassuring me everything will be alright. By the end of the night, I believe him.

Chapter Thirteen

Sarah

Sixty-five days later and I've been moved into his house for a while now. Mira and Teddy know about David's secret, and they are surprisingly okay with it. I quit doing pedicures. Because, frankly, I don't want to be wrangling twin toddlers in my forties while working a job that's giving me carpal tunnel and sore knees if I don't have to. Maybe I'll go back to work when they're older or if David's job doesn't cut it or something, but for now, I'm sitting on eggs and feeling fine.

Wait. Feeling a *crack*. And another one. OH MY GOD. The eggs are cracking!

"David! The eggs are cracking!" I shout toward the kitchen from my spot in the cushy nest we made in the living room.

Pots and pans crash to the floor and footsteps run toward me. David appears from around the corner, feathers sprouting as he comes toward me.

"You're sure? They're coming?"

"Help me up!"

David takes my hands and helps me carefully stand up. Sure enough, both eggs start to crack. I lose my grip on David's hand when his fingers fuse, and it turns into a flipper. *Uh-oh.*

"David, this is not the time," I warn him.

"I'm sorry. I'm just very stressed. What if something goes wrong?" he whines.

"David, calm down. I need you."

"Okay. Okay."

I turn back to watch the eggs crack open, but behind me, I hear a loud series of snaps in succession. *Oh no.* I turn around with a sigh.

"David, terrible timing."

I stand with my hands on my hips, looking down at my tiny, penguin husband. When he gets this stressed, he turns fully into a penguin. An actual penguin-sized penguin, and it takes ages to get him back.

He slaps his flippers up and down near his face in em-barrassment.

"I know, but we really have to work on this. The kids are going to be stressful. They're going to be toddlers. They'll get into all sorts of trouble. I can't have you panicking and going gentoo every time something happens." I cross my arms and think. "Stay here with the eggs for a second while I call Teddy to come help."

David squeaks in fright before hustling over to the eggs, which combined are bigger than he is at the moment. I call Teddy, who answers sleepily after a few rings.

"Teddy, hon, the babies are coming. David turned penguin. Can you come over?"

"What? Of course, Mom. I'd want to see them anyway."

"Okay but–"

"They're gonna be weird, I know. It's okay. I'll love them, Mom. Be right there."

About fifteen minutes later, Teddy arrives. The babies are almost out of the eggs. I want to pull them out, but David said it's important for them to push the shell off of themselves.

"Hey, David," Teddy says as he scratches the top of his penguin head.

David flaps noisily around in a circle, his version of panicking.

"Calm down, they're fine. And the gentoo doctor will be here soon enough to prove it to you." I hear another solid *crack* and peek at the eggs to see the top of one fuzzy head poking out of the egg. "Oh, we've got one."

My baby's here. I chew nervously on my bottom lip as I reach in to pick up my baby. I'm not entirely sure what to expect. Every gentoo baby is different. They can be any-where from fully penguin-featured to fully human-fea-tured when they're born, with any mix of features in be-tween. The mix of features lasts for a few weeks until it settles into the human form, aside from choice or stress. But for now, it could be anything. So, I reach in and pick up my baby.

She's a beautiful baby girl, with pitch-black hair, who just so happens to have one downy penguin flipper instead of a left hand.

"Hello, baby girl. Your name is Sharon. I love you very much. Would you like to see your daddy? He's very small right now. See?" I carefully crouch to David's height so he can see the baby and she can be near him. She slaps him with her tiny flipper, and Teddy and I can't help but laugh. "Here Teddy, will you clean up Slappy? I think I heard another crack."

I was right, the second egg is open, and my next baby girl, Catherine, is ready to come out and face the world. She's a little more on the penguin side than her sister, with her entire bottom half from the waist down being fuzzy baby gentoo.

I'll have to keep both of them hidden from the world until they're able to stay in human form. It will be difficult for years after that even since toddlers apparently think it's funny to shift at inappropriate times. I'll be stuck alone with them for a long time. But Teddy and Mira promise to visit often. And of course, I have David.

He promises to take us to the Falklands for a long vacation when they start to get to the terrible twos so I can catch a break and we can visit some more distant relatives of his.

I'm nervous about the life ahead of me but excited too. It's going to have tough moments, but I'll have David to help me.

Once we get this thing with his panic attacks figured out.

I poke him with the toe of my slipper as he stands there flapping his flippers. He looks at me, and I raise a brow.

"It's time to switch back. You've had enough time to panic. I need you now, David."

It takes a moment, but soon enough he's back. He's doing deep breathing exercises, calming himself down.

"Alright. Sorry about that. I'll work on it, I promise."

"I know you will. You're always a perfect gentleman." Handing him our daughter, I kiss the tip of his nose.

"Gentooman," Teddy says with a laugh.

"Oh no. That was so bad," I say, but can't help but laugh as well.

I watch David holding our little girls, one in each arm. He's telling them about how he met a beautiful goddess on the beach, who saved his life. How that goddess is their mother. He looks up at me and smiles when he realizes I'm watching him, then goes back to telling our girls our love story.

I love him so, so much. I'm so thankful for the unicorn who hit him with a volleyball when he wouldn't try her dating app. She found me my perfect gentooman.

Bonus Chapter
David

*T*akes place around chapter 12.5, returning to when *Sarah was pregnant*

"David, I think I need a biology lesson. I have a lot of questions about this now that the initial excitement has worn off. Am I going to be alright? I'm not *really* going to lay eggs, am I? You can't be serious?"

Sighing, I pull Sarah closer to me on the sofa. It's been a week now and she's already getting plump around the middle. The penguin in me chirps happily.

"The answer's the same as the other dozen times you've asked that question, love. It's the way the genetics of my kind work. Since I'm a gentoo type, and you're a female human, our children will be gentoo and they'll hatch from eggs. If I were a female gentoo and you were a human male, they would be fully human. It's a bit of magical biology for you. Of course, as with regular biology, there's always a dash of chaos thrown in, as there's a lot of ways to be that aren't exactly male or female."

I twirl her hair around my finger, enjoying the closeness of the moment. Usually, it's her educating me daily on just about every topic related to biology, especially when it comes to aquatic creatures. It's nice to be the teacher for once.

"Well, how big are they? If they contain babies they have to be pretty big. How am I supposed to push eggs out of my vagina? They're hard! I'm going to split open!"

"Don't worry about your bits, our women have been doing this for ages and they're just fine." I kiss the top of her head before continuing. "The eggshell is soft and leathery, when the baby is being pushed out, and the babies are smaller than full-term human babies. When the shell hits the air it starts to solidify. I'm not saying birth will be easy by any means—it's still childbirth. It's just not going to be birthing a nine-pound, rock-solid egg if that's what you're worried about."

Sarah blows out a long breath as she relaxes against me.

"I guess that makes sense. Are they going to be little penguins in the egg? Or human-looking babies?"

"Could be either. Or one of each. Most likely a combination of the two. When I was born, for example, I was entirely human other than that I had a beak. Made breastfeeding entirely impossible."

Sarah's laughter shakes my shoulder. It's good to hear it—she's been worried too often lately.

"How long does it last?"

"A few weeks. But we'll have a hard time taking them out in public for quite a long time due to the uncontrollable shifting. We'll have to plan for that." There's silence for a moment. I feel the guilt in my belly that's become familiar again. "I'm so sorry to make you upend your life like this, Sarah. If I could have planned things differently I would have."

"Hey, it's okay." She sits up straight, looks me in the eye, and brushes a hand against my cheek. "If I didn't want to go through with this I would have, you know, ended it. But I love you and I think we're going to be good parents. Plus, my life could use a little upending. Or, in this case, a lot of it."

My lips quirked up at the edges as I trace my thumb along the side of her neck. "I do love when your end is up."

Sarah rolls her eyes and shoves me gently in the center of my chest.

"If that was supposed to be an innuendo, it was terrible," she says.

"I didn't think it was too bad. And anyway, it's true. You, bent over, tail end facing up, makes me—"

"Fish," Sarah interrupts.

"What? That's not where I was headed. Doesn't even make sense." I wrack my brain trying to think of what delightfully deviant act she could be referring to but I can't think of one. I've only been sexually active for a brief time, however. Maybe it's something I just don't know of yet.

"No, fish. I need it. All of a sudden I've got an over-whelming craving. I feel like I'm going to cry if I don't get some. We need sushi. Sashimi. Now." Sarah grabs onto the front of my shirt and pleads with her eyes desperately watering.

"Ah, yeah, it's about time for that I suppose. Fish'll be most of your diet until the babies are born. Get your jacket. It's time for lunch, then we'll head to the market to grab some for dinner. And breakfast."

Her nose scrunches up at the thought of all-day, every-day fish.

"I don't love this for me but I suppose it could be worse. After hearing about hippopotamus mating rituals I think I've got it pretty good."

"What, you don't like being showered with dung?" I ask as I take her hand to help her off the sofa.

"No, not particularly," she says with a laugh.

"I'll stick with showering you with love then."

"That I can handle." She kisses me on the cheek as we walk toward the door. "You're such a sweetie."

A few moments later we're out the door and walking down the front steps, Sarah ahead of me.

"Oh!" Sarah shouts as she starts to fall forward. I catch her just before she has a chance to hit the ground.

"Are you okay?" My heart pounds and my penguin squawks frantically inside me. I can feel my feathers itch under my skin.

"I'm fine. It just scared me. Thank you for catching me." Her face pales when she turns to look at me. "Go back inside, David. Let's order in tonight or something."

"What's wrong?"

"Just go. Hurry."

We head back inside, and as we enter I pass by the mirror near the front entrance. My face is covered in feathers. Ah.

"Damn anxiety," I mumble.

"Is this going to be a problem my whole pregnancy?" Sarah asks.

"Of course not," I reply. "I'm sure I'll have it under control. I wouldn't want to be running around as a little penguin when times were tough, would I?"

Sarah laughs. Then there's a pause where her eyebrow raises.

"Wait, can you turn into a regular-sized penguin just from anxiety? That couldn't happen in times of emergency, could it? That would be *really* inconvenient."

"It's not happened since I was a child so I very highly doubt it. Don't worry, Sarah. It's all under control."

The penguin inside me rustles nervously, still wound up from Sarah's near fall. I can feel the feathers under my skin—can't quite get them to retreat yet. But it's fine. It'll be alright.

It's all under control.

Find Me Again

Find all my information at
https://sylviamorrow.carrd.co
or follow my Amazon profile for the latest releases.